FOURTH GRADE RATS

**Look for these other great books
by Jerry Spinelli**

*Report to the Principal's Office
Do the Funky Pickle
Who Ran My Underwear Up the Flagpole?
Picklemania
The Library Card*

FOURTH GRADE RATS

JERRY SPINELLI

SCHOLASTIC INC.

New York Toronto London Auckland Sydney
Mexico City New Delhi Hong Kong Buenos Aires

ISBN 0-590-44244-9

55 54 53 52 51 50 49 48 47 46 45 ·   4 5 6 7 8 9/0

Printed in the U.S.A.   40

For Bill and Ginny
and
Michael, Leslie and Lonnie
and
my own fourth grade teacher
Elizabeth Coleman
an angel among rats

Contents

1

Rats Don't

"First grade babies!
Second grade cats!
Third grade angels!
Fourth grade . . . RRRRRATS!"

It was the first recess of the first day of school. A mob of third-graders had me and Joey Peterson backed up against the monkey bars.

They were giving us the old chant. When they came to the word "rats," they screamed it in our faces. Then they ran off laughing.

"I wish I was still in third grade," I said.

"Why?" said Joey.

"So I could still be an angel."

"Not me." He climbed onto the first bar. "I waited three years to be a rat." He climbed to the next bar. "And now I *am* a rat."

He climbed to the top bar. He shouted over the school yard: "And proud of it!"

I started to climb. My sneaker slipped on a bar, and I went down instead of up. The first thing I landed on was my hand. My thumb got bent back, way back.

Pain!

I howled. As loud as I could.

It still hurt.

I kicked the ground, the monkey bars, the nearest tree. My thumb still hurt, and so did my foot.

Only one thing left to do. I cried.

Joey's voice came down from the high monkey bar: "Rats don't cry."

The bell rang to end recess.

I jogged, sniffling, to the door. When I got there, Judy Billings was behind me. Like a miracle, the pain in my thumb disappeared.

For me, there was no such thing as pain when Judy Billings was around. I loved her. I was sure that any day she would start to love me back. In the meantime, she mostly ignored me.

But I kept trying. Judy was in the other fourth grade class, so I didn't see too much of her.

When I did, I figured I had to make the most of it.

That's why I held the door open for her. She went through. As usual, she ignored me. I didn't care. For one second, she was inches away. Heaven was a trainload of those seconds.

A little while later, during Silent Reading, a spider crawled onto Becky Hibble's book. Becky screamed and flipped her book into the air. The book landed on the floor. The spider landed in my lap.

Next thing I know, I'm on my desktop, tap dancing and yelling, "Get 'im off me! Get 'im off me!"

On the way to lunch, Joey's whisper came again: "Rats don't get scared of spiders."

We sat together in the lunchroom, just like last year. And we both brought our lunches from home, just like last year.

We sat at our usual table. I opened my lunch box. I was checking out my stuff when I heard Joey snickering. I looked up. He was wagging his head. His face was smirky.

I looked around the lunchroom. "What's funny?"

"That," he said. He was pointing at my lunch box.

"What's wrong with it?" I said.

"Ain't that the same one you had last year?"

"Yeah. So what?"

He snickered again. "Look at it."

I looked at it. "So?"

"What do you see?"

"I see a lunch box. What do you see, a Martian?"

He flipped the cover down. "*Look* at it. What's *on* it? All over it."

I looked again. "Elephants."

He broke out laughing. He pounded the table. His face was red. I had never known I could make him so happy. He tried to talk a couple times — "What — What — " but he kept cracking up. Finally he slapped his hand over his eyes and got it out: "What are they doing?"

"The elephants?"

"Yeah, yeah."

"They're flying."

This time I thought lunch would be over before he stopped laughing. Other kids were looking over. Gerald Willis, a sixth-grader and the school bully, threw a french fry at Joey, but that didn't stop him.

I unwrapped my sandwich. I didn't have all day.

At long last, he took a deep breath. He

said, "Right. Flying elephants. Big flapping ears. Doing yo-yo's with their trunks."

"*Some* of them," I corrected him. "Other ones have fishing poles."

His cheeks bulged with laugh balls, but he swallowed them. "Morton — " He made himself serious. "Don't you get it?"

"Get what?"

"Flying elephants on your lunch box, man. That's little kiddie stuff." He picked up his paper bag. He wagged it in my face. "*This* is what a rat brings his lunch in."

I took a bite of my sandwich. "What do I care?"

"That's just it, man. You oughtta care." He opened his bag. "If you don't care, who will? Your mom probably got you that box, right?"

"Yeah, I guess."

"Right. Moms. They just want to keep you a baby all your life. Suds, I'm telling ya, you gotta put a stop to it now. If you leave it up to your mom, you'll be going off to college with a flying-elephant lunch box."

I looked at my lunch box. I'd had it since first grade, when I was a baby and glad of it. Most of the other kids broke their lunch boxes, or lost them, so they got new ones every year. My lunch box just kept rolling on. The elephants were fading, and some were even starting to look like hippos.

But I loved my lunch box. It was like a brother to me. Now that I thought about it, I wasn't even sure I could eat lunch at school without it. And as for my lunch box going off to college with me someday — well, to tell you the truth, I didn't see anything so bad about that.

I looked at Joey. He was wagging his head and smirking again.

Uh-oh, I thought, it's not just the lunch box.

2

Real Meat

"Okay," I said, "now what?"

He pointed. "That."

"My sandwich?"

"You gonna eat peanut butter and jelly all your life?"

"Why not?" I said. "I like it." I took another bite.

He sneered. "Yeah, right. I can see it now. You're in this big fancy restaurant with all these fancy, big-shot business people, and everybody orders their dinners, and the waitress comes to you and you go, 'Duh, I'll have the peanut-butter-and-jelly sandwich, please.' Right, Morton. They're really gonna be impressed."

"So what am I supposed to be eating?"

He laid his sandwich on the table. He opened it up.

"Baloney?"

"Meat, Morton, meat."

"I eat meat," I told him.

"Real meat, Morton? Ever eat a steak?"

I thought about it. "I don't know. Maybe once."

"Ever eat a pork chop? A roast beef? A *liver*?"

I put my sandwich down. "You're ruining my lunch."

He looked proud. "I ate a bite of liver last night."

"You're lying."

"Swear to God."

"You didn't get sick?"

"Nope."

"How'd it taste?" I shuddered at the thought.

He made a face. "Terrible."

"Terrible? So why'd you eat it? You're stupider than I thought."

"Not as stupid as wanting to be an angel baby all my life. You wanna grow up, you gotta eat stuff you don't like. And I'll tell you something else." He leaned across the table, getting real serious. "It's an idea of mine. The worse it tastes, the faster you grow up."

Now it was my turn to laugh. "Yeah, right,

Peterson. All I gotta do is go find a dead skunk and eat it and, poof, I'll be thirty years old."

He slapped his sandwich back together and took a chomp out of it. "Forget it, man. You wanna be a baby, go be a baby." He went on chomping.

I didn't feel like having a fight. I said, "Okay, maybe I'll ask my mom to make me a baloney sandwich one of these days."

"I don't care," he shrugged.

"Say," I said, "where does baloney come from, anyway?" I was trying to picture herds of balonies roaming around on ranches.

I never got an answer. The bell rang.

We packed up our lunches. We didn't even get to eat most of them. As we headed out, I wondered if anybody was looking at my lunch box.

At the door we bumped into Mrs. Simms. She was my third grade teacher. I really liked her. She never exactly said so, but I think I was her favorite student. I hadn't seen her since school ended, back in June.

"Suds Morton!" she went. "How's my big fourth-grader?" She held out her arms.

One thing about Mrs. Simms — she gets physical. If she decides she wants to hug you, there's not much you can do about it. So I just walked

into those arms and let them wrap around me.

"How are they treating you up there?" she said.

"Well, the teacher's okay," I said.

She backed off. She looked at me. "You mean something's *not* okay?"

I felt squirmy. "Well, it's not as much fun being a rat."

At first she didn't understand. Then she got a big smile. "Now, don't be so glum. Before you know it, fourth grade will be over, and you'll be a — what's fifth grade?"

"Monkeys," I told her.

"Of course, monkeys. You'll be a monkey." She hugged me again. She whispered, "And don't forget, you'll *always* be an angel to me."

She laughed and sent me on my way.

In the hallway, I felt a hand on top of my head. Was Mrs. Simms following me? I turned. It was Gerald Willis, who was *born* a rat. His lips were puckered. They were making kissy noises at me. "Ouuu, little Sudsie, my little teacher's pet. Where's my apple? Didn't you bring me an apple today?"

Before I could do anything, he swiped at my lunch box. The cover sprang open and everything fell to the floor — my half-eaten pea-nut-butter-and-jelly sandwich, my pack of pretzels, my cupcake and . . . my apple.

I scrambled after the stuff on my hands and knees. Kids' feet were everywhere. Somebody crunched my pretzels. As I reached for the apple, a big dirty sneaker kicked it down the hallway. Above me, Gerald Willis was howling.

I was the last one back to the room. I stashed my lunch box and sat down. A note was waiting for me. From Joey. It said: "Swings after school."

I looked over at him. I nodded.

3
Number One

Our school yard has two tire swings. The tires hang on ropes from a bar. You just plunk your rear end on a tire and swing. Or just sit, if you want.

The tires hang almost to the ground. That's so the littlest kids in school can climb onto them.

And that's the situation me and Joey walked into after school. We were going to powwow at the tire swings, but two little kids were already there. They looked like first-graders.

"Guess we'll have to find another place," I said to Joey.

"Guess *they'll* have to find another place," Joey said.

He lifted one of the first-graders out of his

tire, plunked him on the ground, and sat in the tire himself.

The first-grader's face got red. His ears got red. "You rat!" he yelled.

Joey nodded and smirked. "You got that right, kid."

All eyes swung to me. Would I do the same as Joey?

The kid on the other tire looked feistier than her pal. From the look in her eyes, you might have thought she was a ten-foot cat and I was a mouse.

Nobody got a chance to see what I would do, because suddenly the kid bolted. Tore out of there and left the tire swaying on the rope. I realized she may have looked feisty, but she was scared.

The other kid took off, too. But not before he yelled, "Rat!" and spit at me. Missed by a mile. First-graders are not good spitters.

"Sit down," said Joey.

I sat on the tire. "I don't feel right about that," I said.

"About what?"

"About kicking those little kids out."

I kept seeing the girl's eyes as she ran. It was the first time anyone had ever been afraid of me. I couldn't figure out how I felt about it.

"Suds," Joey said, "remember a couple summers ago? Fourth of July? At the park?"

"What about it?" I said.

"The talent show?"

"Yeah."

"The bench?"

"Huh?"

Joey got off his tire. He stood in front of me. "The *bench* we were sitting on to watch the talent show? That we didn't sit on for very long?"

"Oh, yeah . . ." It was coming back to me. "Some kids kicked us off it."

"Fourth-graders," he said. "They *dumped* us off. They lifted one end of the bench — real high — so you and me slid off, onto the ground."

I laughed, picturing Joey and me zooming down the bench like it was a sliding board. "Man, I forgot all about that."

"I didn't," said Joey. He wasn't laughing.

"So," I said, "now that I'm a fourth-grade rat, I'm supposed to go around dumping little kids off benches. Is that it?"

"There's more to it than that," he said.

I starting swinging. "I'm all ears."

Joey got back on his tire. He matched his swinging to mine.

"Suds," he said, "you're in fourth grade now.

That makes you a rat. Stop fighting it. It's nature's way.''

"I can fight it if I want."

"Yeah? How?"

I thought for a minute. "I'll do rotten in school. I'll do so rotten, they'll have to flunk me back to third grade."

"Forget it, dude. You can't go backwards. Time marches on."

"I *liked* being an angel."

Joey stopped his swing. He reached over and stopped mine. "Suds, you ant brain. Angels finish last. What did you ever get out of it, huh? Did anybody ever say, 'Oh, thank you, Suds. You're so nice. You're such an angel.' Huh? Anybody ever say that?"

"Not exactly," I had to admit.

"Your mother ever say, 'Oh, Suds, you're such an angel, you don't have to clean your room anymore'?"

"Guess not."

"Are you allowed to stay up late?"

"No."

"Are you allowed to go anywhere you want by yourself?"

"No."

"Are you allowed to say no to your mom?"

" 'Course not."

He poked my tire. "See. That's what I'm talking about."

"I'm glad *you* know what you're talking about," I said, "because *I* sure don't."

"I'm talking about growing up," he said. "I'm talking about not being an angel baby anymore. I'm talking about taking care of Number One for a change."

I felt stupid, but I had to ask. "Who's this Number One?"

He pointed. "You, dude. You're Number One, for you. I'm Number One for me."

Number One. That sounded good. Maybe there was something to this rat business, after all.

"But what about crying?" I said. "Why can't I cry or be scared of spiders?"

He got off his tire. He faced me. He was dead serious. "Because real men don't cry."

"What's men got to do with it? Before, you said it's rats that don't cry."

"That's right," he said. "That's the whole point. Being a rat is the next step up to being a man. You want to be a man, don't you?"

"Sure," I said. "I guess so."

"Well," he said, "you can't be a man without being a rat first." He poked me in the chest. "That's what fourth grade is all about."

Except for us, the school yard was empty. Parents were calling their kids in to dinner.

We headed home. As I walked up the driveway to my house, Joey said, "See ya, rat."

"See ya," I said.

Before I reached the door, he rushed back. He grabbed my arm. "Don't forget," he whispered. "Say no to your mom."

4

Zippernose and Bubba

I'm no good at hiding my feelings. My mother says I would never make a good poker player, whatever that means.

"Bad first day?" she said as soon as she spotted me.

I slumped on the sofa. "Worst first day ever."

She whistled. "That *is* bad. What happened?"

"I don't know. Lots. It's hard to explain."

She sat down beside me. She patted my knee. "Give it a try."

I took a deep breath. "Well, it's all about being in fourth grade now. You know, a rat? Third grade angels, fourth grade rats? So I'm not an angel anymore."

She snapped her fingers. "Well, golly gee, you coulda fooled me."

"You're not funny, Mom."

"That's *your* opinion. I happen to think I am *quite* funny."

I glared at her. "Yeah? Well, you wouldn't think it was so funny if *you* were in fourth grade and everybody was giving you a hard time. Life isn't as simple as it was in the old days, you know. I got *problems*."

Her grin disappeared. Her eyes changed. She stroked my hair. "Yeah, I guess you do. Tell you what." She squeezed my leg. "I think it's time for a bath."

"Yeah," I said. "I think so, too."

I dragged myself upstairs.

When I was a baby, I had upset stomachs a lot. It made me pretty cranky. "You were not a ton of fun to be with," my mother says.

But she discovered something that helped — a bath. The warm water would have a good effect on me. I would stop crying. I would calm down. Sometimes she would pour in bubble bath. Pretty soon I'd be laughing and splashing. Suds were flying.

My mother says each time a bubble burst on

my face, it made a freckle. She says suds gave me my curly hair, too.

One thing's for sure, suds gave me my name.

I stopped having upset stomachs by the time I was two. But I never stopped liking a warm bath. It doesn't matter what time of the day or night it is. If I'm sad or ticked off or wound up about something, I usually feel better if I head for the water.

Well, that's what she meant when she told me to take a bath. Five minutes later, there I was, in the tub with my tugboat and my dinosaur.

I guess even I had to admit that I was getting a little too old for toys in the bathtub. But I still liked them. They've been with me as long as I can remember. What was I supposed to do? All of a sudden hate them? Throw them away?

I started thinking about my life, the important things in it. My Disney World T-shirt. My bike. My Klondike bars. My Matchbox car collection. Heavenly hash ice cream. Sliding boards. Spiderman. Spikerkid. Winky, my one-eyed teddy bear, my oldest friend in the world.

I tried to picture life without them. I couldn't.

I always thought when you grew up, stuff like bikes and bubble gum just sort of disappeared from your life. You didn't want them any-

more. They got replaced by cars and coffee and
all.

I never thought you actually had to give them
up, whether you were ready to or not. I thought
growing up was just something that happened.
You just sort of went along for the ride. But if
Joey was right, growing up didn't just happen
to you — you had to *work* at it. And that,
according to Joey, meant being a rat.

For the first time in my life, I wanted time to
slow down. I didn't care if I never had another
birthday, as long as I could keep my one-eyed
teddy bear.

My brain was sore from all this thinking. I ran
the faucet some more. I let myself sink into the
water. The lower I sank, the better I felt. It was
like I could feel time slowing down . . . feel it
stopping . . . going backwards . . . back to third
grade angels . . . second grade cats . . . first
grade babies . . . little yellow tugboats bobbing
in the water . . . bobbing . . . bobbing. . .

My mother's voice: "Sudsie! Dinnertime!"

As soon as I sat down to dinner, Zippernose —
otherwise known as my sister, Amy — sneered
at me: "Rat."

She didn't stop there. She puckered her
mouth and raised her upper lip, baring her two

front teeth. I had to admit, it was a good imitation. "Rat — rat — rat," she went.

My mother plopped some mashed potatoes on her plate. "Amy, stop."

It was too late. Baby brother Bubba was already baring his little fangs and going, "Wat — wat — wat." He doesn't say his *r*'s right yet.

"Bubba, you, too," snapped my mother.

Right, Mom.

Now Zippernose was nibbling like a rat on a slice of bread.

And now Bubba was nibbling like a rat on his hot dog.

And now my mother was standing and slamming a serving spoon down on the table. "I said stop!" She glared at my father. "Elmore?"

My father looked up from his plate. "Stop," he said, and went back to his eating.

My mother is pretty laid back, but compared to my father, she's a nervous wreck.

My mother sat back down.

"Mom," whined Zippernose, "I can't help it. He's a rat now. I'm just treating him like the dirty, rotten, slimy rat that he is."

"Wat — wat — wat," said Bubba.

"E-*nough*!" commanded my mom. "Amy, another word from you and you can leave the table."

Zippernose's words stopped, but not her faces. She kept baring her front teeth and nibbling on her food.

"All *right*," said Mom. "Upstairs."

Zippernose screeched. "Mom — I didn't say *anything*."

"You're making faces."

"You said not another *word*. You didn't say not another *face*."

"I'm saying it now. Your dinner is over. Leave the table. Upstairs. To your room. Close the door. Good night."

Zippernose stomped off. Before she ran upstairs, she yelled back, "Rodent!"

Bubba echoed: "Wodent — wodent — wodent!"

Then he started laughing. When Bubba laughs and eats at the same time, he becomes a midget volcano. Pieces of mashed potato and hot dog were flying everywhere.

I slammed my fork down. "I'm outta here."

I stomped off.

My mother called, "Suds, here!"

I didn't say no, like Joey told me. But I didn't say yes, either. I just kept going.

5

You're Not Funny

Later, my mother cornered me in my room.

"Okay," she said, "is that how dinner is going to be every day? A madhouse?"

"It's not my fault," I told her. "All I did was get promoted to fourth grade."

My mother sat on the bed. "Sudsie, maybe you're taking this too seriously. It's just a school kids' rhyme, you know. I'm sure it'll pass over in a day or two."

"Sure," I sneered, "tell that to all the kids at school calling me a rat. Tell it to Zippernose. Tell it to Joey."

"What does Joey say about all this?"

I laughed. "Hah. He loves it. He's glad he's a

25

rat. He says it's nature's way. He says it's a step up to being a man."

She chuckled. "The way to a man is through a rat, huh?"

"I keep telling you it's not funny."

"You're right," she said. She spanked her own hand. "There. Bad Mom. That'll teach me."

I glared at her. "You can forget it if you're trying to make me laugh. It's not working."

She pretended to pout. "Darn. Okay, no more funny stuff. You're miserable and that's that, right?"

"Right."

"Bath didn't help?"

"Yeah, it did, till I had to get out."

She snapped her fingers. "Ah-*hah*! All *right*. I'll tell you what we're going to do. I'm going to call the school and pull you out of there. We'll hire a tutor to come in and teach you. She can sit on the toilet seat while you're in the tub. We'll serve you your meals there. After a couple months, you should be shriveled down to the size of, oh, a frog."

I pointed to the door. "Mom — out."

"Or maybe we could put wheels on the bathtub and roll you off to school each day. We could — "

"MOM!"

She shut up. She stood. She was biting her lip to keep from cracking up at her own hilarious self.

She took a deep breath. She put her hand on my shoulder. "Tell you what. There's more than one way to become a man."

"What's that?" I said.

"Go sweep the sidewalk. You'll be a man in no time."

She looked at me. I looked at her. Joey's voice hissed in my ear: *Say no to your mother.*

Joey's voice was no match for my mother's look.

I got the broom and went outside. I swept the sidewalk.

My father had just cut the grass. He was putting the mower back in the garage. His weights were in the corner. They were covered with dust.

"Dad," I said, "do you still lift your weights?"

"Haven't for a couple years now," he said. "I'm saving them for you and Bubba."

"Did they help you become a man?"

He looked at them. "Oh, I don't know. I guess they helped me look like one."

"Can I see your muscle?"

He wheeled the mower into its place. He laughed. "You've haven't asked me that in a long time. You used to ask me every day.''

I lifted his arm to get him started. "Well, come on, let me see.''

He put his hand behind his head and made the muscle. It looked like a baseball in there, or even a softball.

"Make it bounce," I told him.

He made it bounce.

I reached up and touched it. It was smooth and round and hard, like wood.

"Pull me up," I said, "like you used to."

He lowered his arm a little. "I don't know if I still can. You're not such a shrimp anymore, you know.''

I grabbed on with both hands. "Hoist away!''

His arm started to crank up. My legs got straight, then I was on tiptoes, then I was off the ground. I hung there for a couple seconds, then he let me down.

We went back out. He closed the garage door.

I asked him if he used to take a lunch box to school when he was in fourth grade.

He thought. He nodded. "Yep, I did.''

"Did it have anything on the outside of it?''

"Nope. It was one of those old-fashioned ones, like Grandpop took to work. I wanted one just like his.''

"No animals on it, huh? Elephants? Anything?"

He shook his head. "No, 'fraid not. It was black. About as dull as a lunch box gets."

He opened the front door.

"How about swings, Dad? Did you ever kick a little kid off a swing?"

He stopped. He looked at me funny. "Where did that question come from? Somebody kick you off a swing?"

"Oh, no," I said, heading inside. "Just wondering."

When I pulled down my bedcover that night, I found a mousetrap on my pillow. (Dad thought we had a mouse once.) It was set with a little piece of cheese. I tripped it with a pencil. It snapped like a cap pistol and flipped halfway up to the ceiling. I grabbed the trap, charged down the hall to Zippernose's room, yanked open her door, and rifled the trap into the dark, right about where she would be lying in bed.

The phone rang. I didn't bother with the squawks coming from Zippernose's room. I picked up the phone. A voice whispered: "Did you say no to your mother?"

6

Joey Becomes a Man

Nothing much changed during the next couple days.

First-graders called fourth-graders "Rats!" Fourth-graders bared their front teeth and snarled. First-graders ran away squealing.

I kept opening doors for Judy Billings.

Judy Billings kept ignoring me.

By the second week of school, the first-graders were tired of the game. And without the first-graders calling them "Rats!" the fourth-graders pretty much forgot that's what they were.

Except for Joey Peterson.

Joey was doing just what he'd said, taking care of Number One. I don't mean he went around kicking people in the kneecaps. I mean he did things pretty much his own way. He didn't care what anyone else thought.

One day in class we had pretend elections, to learn how government works. Joey nominated himself for President of the United States. Then he voted for himself.

He even looked different. He got his hair cut practically down to the nubs. "Like Marine boot camp," he said. And he started wearing one of his father's old sweatbands around his head. He got a black marker and wrote "No. 1" on it.

Joey was on his way to becoming a man. In fact, I think I saw him become a man before my very eyes. On a Thursday at the school yard.

It was after lunch. We were just cruising around when a bee started flying near us. I hate bees, as much as I hate spiders. So I took off, flapping my hands.

I heard Joey call: "Suds — look."

I turned. "What?"

"*Look.*"

He was holding out his arm.

I couldn't see anything. "Look at what?"

He was keeping very still, staring at his arm. "Come closer."

I came closer — and I saw. The bee was on his arm, crawling up and down.

Gave me the shakes just to watch. "Swat 'im," I whispered.

He just kept staring at the bee.

By now, other kids were coming over, gawking. One of them was Gerald Willis, the school thug.

When Willis saw what was happening, he snuck up behind Joey and knocked Joey's arm from underneath. Joey's arm jerked up, and the bee took off.

But not for long. The bee made a U-turn and came right back and — *zap* — stung Joey right on his arm.

Kids shrieked. I think a couple of little ones fainted. Everybody rushed forward. A bee sting! Next to a car door slamming on your hand, probably the most painful thing in the world. Major agony.

I tunneled through the mob. Would Joey be in convulsions? Conscious? Alive?

He was grinning. He was staring at the little, white bee-sting bump on his arm, and he was *grinning*.

He was a rat. He was a man.

Girls swarmed over him.

"Ouu, Joey, it must hurt so *bad*. How can you *stand* it?"

"Ouu, Joey, don't you want to *cry*?"

"Ouu, Joey, you're so *brave*."

"Ouu, *Joey*."

One of the girls was Judy Billings.

Judy Billings followed Joey around the rest of the day like a puppy dog. I walked home with him, but so did she, and it was like I wasn't even there.

"Joey, can I see it?"

(For the millionth time.)

"Ouu, it gives me the shivers."

(It's not even visible.)

"Weren't you *scared*? I heard people can *die* from bee stings."

(Hey, look at me. I'm the one dying around here.)

"You think we ought to go the emergency ward?"

(Barf!)

"Can I see it just one more time?"

(Scream!)

Of course, she couldn't just look at it with her eyes. She had to look at it with her hands, too. I guess she had little eyeballs in her fingertips.

First she would touch the invisible sting spot and say, "Does that hurt?" And Joey would say, "No." Then she would press it and go, "Does *that* hurt?" And Joey would look all cool and say, "Nah."

Of course, that wasn't enough for her. She had to start feeling around the rest of his arm, to see if it was swelling up. She said it was. He said it wasn't.

So of course, she *had* to switch over to his other arm and go feeling around that one, to see how it compared. And all of a sudden, it wasn't about a bee sting anymore.

"Wow, your muscles are so hard."

She didn't even see him clenching his arm. Girls are so dumb about that.

"Do you lift weights?" she cooed.

"I lift my father's barbells," I said, crossing my fingers.

She gave him a look, like, Did you hear a voice? Is somebody else here?

As for Joey himself, he was a little hard to figure. I had to admit, he wasn't exactly sucking up to her. He was letting her do the talking.

In fact, for a minute there it even looked like he was trying to help me. He gave me a little jab and said to her, "Hey, I happen to know another guy that has pretty good muscles, too."

"Not as good as yours," she cooed.

"Oh, yeah," he said. "Even better than mine. And you know what? I think he likes you."

Her eyes widened. "Really?"

"Yeah, really. And I bet you'd like him, too."

"Maybe I would."

She was blushing. I was blushing. Things were looking up. I was feeling *good*.

Joey shot me a quick grin. "Want me to tell you who it is?"

My face was burning. *Tell her. Don't tell her. Tell her. Don't tell her.*

She gave him a shy smile. "You don't have to."

"I don't?" he said.

"No."

"How's that?"

"Because I already know who it is."

I was ready to faint. I wanted to crawl under the nearest car.

Joey poked me again. "Yeah? Who do you think it is?"

She giggled. She blushed even redder. She looked up and down the street. She cupped her hands and whispered into his ear. When she pulled away, she giggled again. He just gawked at her. She whispered some more in his ear. Then she ran off giggling down the street.

We walked. Joey didn't say anything, so I did. "Well?"

"Well, what?"

"Well, who did she say?"

He shrugged. "Ah, nothing."

I grabbed his shirt and jerked him to a stop. "Peterson, who did she say?"

He sniffed. He shrugged. He looked away. "Me."

"You?"

"Yeah. She thought I was making it up about somebody else liking her, 'cause I was afraid to say it was me."

I let his shirt go. "Oh, great. Good friend you are."

He screeched. "What could I do? I was trying to help ya."

"Yeah, big help. I didn't hear you telling her she was wrong. I didn't hear you say you *don't* like her."

"I don't. You know it. You can have her all you want."

"Traitor," I said.

"Suds — "

"Traitor."

I went to the other side of the street.

After a while he called. "Suds, it's Friday. Stay over my house tonight."

"Never," I said.

7

Trashing Joey's Room

When I got to Joey's house that night, his room looked the same as always. But not for long.

"Been working on myself so far," he said. "Now it's my room's turn."

First we put up posters. Rambo. Hulk Hogan. And one showing this big, nasty, robot-type dude, except you could see whiskers and a long tail sticking out. It was called "Robo Rat."

He checked out the walls. "Good. Now the rest."

He started with his bookshelf. He pulled out four or five volumes from his encyclopedia and threw them on the floor. Then he tossed out a couple comic books and a *National Geographic*.

He opened every drawer in his dresser. He flipped out stuff from each one — socks, underwear, shirts. They landed all over. He kicked his

wastebasket over. He dragged his dirty clothes
hamper from the closet and dumped it on the
floor. He charged into his desk. Pencils and
papers and rubber bands went flying. About the
only thing he didn't do was spit.

By now, you could hardly see the floor. He
stood in the middle, turning, nodding, smiling.
"Yeah. Now it's *my* room."

I just sat on the bed, stunned. Until then Joey
Peterson's room had been the neatest room I
had ever seen.

And he wasn't done. We ordered a pizza, and
when he got down to the crust of each slice, he
tossed it over his shoulder. One landed in his
underwear drawer. The pizza box he flipped like
a Frisbee against a wall.

After that, we had Fudgsicles and Peanut
Chews. The wrappers — at least, his wrappers — went onto the floor. He took a wad of
bubble gum from his mouth and winged it
against his dresser mirror. It stuck.

I guess he couldn't think of anything else to
do to his room, because he turned back to
himself. He pulled something from his pocket.
It looked like a little notepad.

"What is it?" I asked him.

He grinned. "Tattoos."

"Oh, no."

Into the bathroom we went. He tore off four and wetted them. Pretty soon he was tattooed on the chest (skull and crossbones), both arms (a cobra and a mongoose), and rear end ("If You Can Read This, You're Too Close").

"You know they're not gonna last," I told him.

"They'll last till I get a bath," he said. "And I ain't getting a bath 'cept once a month from now on."

I pinched my nose. "Oh, great, man. Do you have to *smell* like a rat, too?"

As we left the bathroom, we bumped into his mother. "I saw your room," she said. "What are you doing in there, training elephants?"

We laughed.

"Well" — she looked at Joey — "as soon as Suds leaves tomorrow, you see that it gets cleaned up."

Uh-oh, I thought. This is it. Will he practice what he preaches?

Joey slouched against the bathroom doorway. He looked off down the hall. "Nah, I don't think so."

Mrs. Peterson blinked. "You don't think what?"

"I don't think I'm gonna clean it up. I like it that way."

I took a step back. If Mrs. Peterson was about

to get violent, I wanted to be out of range. Joey looked at the floor. I looked at Mrs. Peterson. Mrs. Peterson glared daggers at Joey. This lasted for about three hours.

Then all of a sudden it was over. Mrs. Peterson gave a little shrug and a smile and said, "Okay," and walked away.

I gawked at Joey. Just on this one day, he had faced a bee and a mad mother, and here he was, alive and healthy as ever.

He gave me a thumbs-up sign. "See? Nothin' to it."

Then Joey told me to wait in his room. When he came back, he had a hammer, a jar of nails, a bag of cotton balls, a bottle of iodine, and some Band-Aids.

I asked what all that was for.

"Put a hole in my ear," he said.

I screeched. "You're gonna wear an *earring*?"

"Nope."

"So why are you putting a hole in your ear?"

He grinned. "Pain."

If I didn't already know he was looney, I knew it now.

I told him, "The only thing about you that's turning rat is your brain."

He ignored me. He cleared a space on his

desk. He opened the jar of nails and dumped them out. He rooted through them until he found one he liked: a long, thin one.

He handed the nail to me, along with the hammer. He got a felt-tip pen, went to his mirror, and put a dot in the middle of his right earlobe. He came back to the desk, knelt down beside it, real close, and flapped his lobe out so it sat like a tiny pancake on the top edge of the desk.

I looked at the hammer and nail in my hands. "Oh, no," I said. I dumped them on the desk and took a seat on the bed. "*You* do it, if you're crazy enough."

"I would," he said, "but I can't, not like this. C'mon. Just do it."

I didn't move. "You mind if I ask you a stupid question? Like why you want to hammer a hole in your ear? What do you mean, pain?"

He pulled his earlobe off the desk. He sat on the floor. "You gotta learn to take pain, that's all. No more crybaby. You know, like the Indians used to do. You had to go through stuff, really painful, before you could become a man. You had to prove you could take it."

"I got news for you," I told him. "You're not an Indian."

He looked at me, disgusted. He grabbed the hammer and held it out. "You gonna do it?"

I shook my head no.

He threw the hammer down. "Thanks, pal."

"Listen," I said, "if it means that much to you, why don't you just do some easier kind of pain? Something you don't need a hammer and nail for."

"Like what?" he said.

I thought about it. "Well . . . how about bending your finger back?"

"Nah," he said. "That's dorky."

I thought some more. "How about kicking your door with your bare big toe?"

He didn't like that one, either.

"I got it!" I said. "I knuckle your head ten times."

"Forget it."

But now I didn't want to forget it. I was getting into it. I rattled off some more: "Pull out a hair. . . . Sit the three thickest volumes of the encyclopedia on your tongue. . . . Sleep all night with erasers up your nose. . . . Wrap your mouth around the doorknob and slam it shut. . . ."

I was still going when the phone rang. It was pretty late, so we were both surprised when his mother called and said it was for him. He went out.

When he came back, he looked innocent. Too innocent.

"It was her, wasn't it?" I said.

"I told her not to call people so late."

I shoved him. "Traitor."

He shoved me back. "Listen, Morton, I didn't call her. She called me."

"Took you long enough to hang up."

"Wha'd you want me to do, slam down the phone as soon as she said hello?"

"Maybe I want you to lay off her."

He laughed. "I keep telling you, jerkface, I don't *care* about her. I ain't chasing her. *She's* chasing *me*. You want her to chase *you*" — he threw the pad of tattoos in my face — "do something about it."

We glared at each other. He turned on the TV. We watched a couple horror movies. In silence. We went to bed.

When we woke up Saturday morning, I said, "Okay."

He rubbed sleepies from his eyes. "Okay what?"

"What do I do?"

He sat up. "You're ready to be a rat?"

I shrugged. "I guess so. But I don't think I know how. It doesn't come natural to me."

"No sweat," he said. "We just do what all beginners do."

"What's that?"

"Practice."

8

Training Camp

We headed for my house. Training camp.

Joey was my coach.

"First," he said, "that crybaby stuff. Gotta go."

"How?" I said.

"You still have your *E.T.*, don't you?"

"Sure." My parents had given me the video-tape movie for my birthday.

"I'll bet you start bawling every time E.T. dies, don't you?"

"Well . . . "

"Follow me."

We stuck my *E.T.* cassette in our VCR and ran it FAST FORWARD to where E.T. dies, or everybody thinks he dies.

As usual, the waterworks came on. My eyes, my cheeks were like Niagara Falls.

Joey punched REWIND, STOP, PLAY. E.T. died again. I cried again.

So it went. Time after time.

Until, on the twenty-second try, Joey ran his fingertip across my cheek and nodded. "Dry." He turned on the light and got in my face like a doctor. "Your eyes are a little watery, but nothing's falling out of them."

He held out his hand. "You're on your way, rat."

I gave him five.

Next was spiders.

Joey found one, trapped it in a paper cup, and brought it to me. I was sweating and shaking.

"Hold out your hand," he said.

"I can't," I told him.

"You want Judy Billings to like you or not?"

"W-what if it's a b-black w-widow?" I shuddered.

"It's not."

"Or a tarantula?"

"It's a little white house spider. Hold out your hand."

"I can't. It won't move."

Joey made it move. He grabbed my hand and dumped the spider onto it.

He was right. It *was* a little white house spider. But to me it *looked* like a tarantula. I screamed and flipped it away.

When we got to the ninth little white house spider, I was still flipping, but I was doing it silently.

Joey sighed. "Well, at least we got rid of that scream."

He clapped his hands. "Okay — up to the roof."

"No," I said.

"Move," he said.

I went upstairs like I was walking to the gallows. Even more than spiders, I'm scared of high places.

Joey steered me to my bedroom window. He made me open it. "Out," he said.

"No," I said.

Outside my window is the roof of our front porch.

"No *way*," I said. I sat on my bed.

I finally agreed to do it under two conditions: (1) I take off my shoes and socks to get a better grip on the roof, (2) we tie me to a rope. We tied one end of the rope to the bed. The other

end, good and tight, went around my chest, under my arms.

I climbed out. I sat on my windowsill.

"Out," he said. "To the edge."

I lowered myself from the sill. I sat on the roof. I dug my fingers and toes and rear end into the pebbly shingles. I inched forward. My heart felt like an exploding football in my chest.

I was halfway to the edge when the sidewalk below started to get wavy. Then the bushes got fuzzy. Then everything was turning around like the inside of a clothes dryer. . . .

Next thing I knew, I was hanging off the edge of the porch roof, swinging in the air above the front steps.

Just then Zippernose came out. The look on her face said: I'm imagining I see my brother hanging from the roof. I'm having a hallucination.

"Call somebody!" I told her. "Get me down from here!"

She half turned, ready to obey me for the first time in her life. Then she spotted my feet. My *bare* feet. This time the look on her face said: I may never get this chance again as long as I live.

She rushed me. She grabbed my legs in a bear hug and started tickling the bottoms of my feet.

We — the Mortons — are a ticklish family. Extremely. By the time my mother finally came out and chased Zippernose off and got me down, I was about dead from laughing.

For my next test, Joey led me to the little kids' playground at the park.

"What're we doing here?" I asked him.

"You'll see," he said.

We waited, watching the little kids.

After a while, Joey said, "You hungry?"

"A little," I said.

"For a Twinkie?"

"Yeah!"

Spongy cake. Creamy inside. I love them.

"Go for it," said Joey.

He pointed to a little kid. He was eating a Twinkie with one hand. The other hand held another Twinkie.

"He don't need two," Joey whispered.

"I can't," I said.

"Take care of Number One."

"I can't."

"Judy Billings . . . Judy Billlllllll-ings . . ."

The kid was passing us. I reached out. I snatched the uneaten Twinkie. The kid howled bloody murder. I shoved the Twinkie back in his hand and took off.

Last test.
Last chance.
We hung around my room, waiting for my mother to ask me to do something. "When she does," Joey said, "you know what to say."

Sure enough, pretty soon my mom showed up. She said, "Suds, will you excuse yourself from Joey long enough to empty your wastebasket, please."

Silence. Joey waiting. My mother waiting. Judy Billings waiting. The world waiting.

I couldn't stand it. Maybe if she hadn't smiled. Maybe if she hadn't said please.

I said, "Okay, Mom."

As soon as my mother left the room, Joey gave a disgusted grunt. He pointed to my one-eyed teddy bear. "I guess you're not gonna throw that baby thing away, either, are you?"

I looked at the bear, at him, in shock.

"Nah, I didn't think so," he sneered. "Better forget it, Morton. You'll never hack it as a rat." He got up and left.

I emptied my basket. I figured he was right. I figured I was dumping my chances with Judy Billings out with my trash.

But I didn't figure on what happened Monday at school.

9

You Want a Rat?

It was lunchtime. I took my tray through the food line. As usual, I waited for Joey.

As I was waiting, I saw a sight that made my eyes pop. Judy Billings was sitting a couple tables away — by herself. Usually she was surrounded by girlfriends.

Judy Billings. Alone. I couldn't believe it.

And I couldn't pass up the chance.

Walking over to her table was as scary as walking on a roof. But I did it.

I sat down next to her. "Hi," I said. "Mind if I sit here?"

She kept looking at her grilled cheese sandwich. "Yes," she said.

I giggled. I grinned. I was thrilled. *Yes*. It

was the first word she ever spoke to me. I'd remember it forever. *Yes. Yes. Yes.*

"I *said* I mind," she said.

"Oh," I said.

What should I do? I was in too deep to back out now.

"Okay," I said. I got up and sat down on the other side of her. "This better?"

"No."

She kept speaking to the grilled cheese sandwich. Did she think I was the sandwich?

I felt my chair move. I looked up — into the face of Gerald Willis. He was pulling my chair backwards. When it was away from the table, he tipped it forward. I slid off to the floor.

It was the bench at the talent show all over again. Only worse.

I got up. I slunk away. Kids were laughing. One of them was a third grade angel, eating a piece of chocolate cake. I didn't take the cake from the angel's hand. I just shoved his hand, cake and all, into his face. Then I mashed them around.

The whole joint was howling.

As I walked out of school that day, Judy Billings happened to be right behind me. This time I didn't hold the door open for her. I let it shut in her face.

I went straight home and up to my room. With one swipe of my hand, I sent my whole Matchbox car collection flying from the top of my bookcase. I probably would have destroyed my room right then if I hadn't headed for the bathtub.

No tugboat and dinosaur this time. Just me and the water. I didn't turn it off till it was up past my belly button. I sank into it as deep as I could. I wanted to pull it over me like a blanket. I wanted to forget the day. I wanted to forget fourth grade.

By the time I got out, I thought I was feeling better. I was wrong. As soon as I got back to my room, I punched Winky, my bear.

At dinner, Zippernose smirked and sneered and snickered until my mother finally said, "What *is* it?"

"I can't tell," giggled Zippernose. "I'll get in trouble."

"If you don't stop that carrying on, you'll *be* in trouble."

"Okay, I'll tell."

My mother looked at me. "I'm not sure I even want to know now. I'll let Suds tell me later if he wants to."

"No!" screeched Zippernose. "I *wanna* tell!"

And before anyone could stop her, she told. About Gerald Willis and the chair. About the third-grader and the cake in the face. About the whole place laughing.

Bubba was going into spasms over the cake scene. My parents just stared at me. My mother looked hurt. "That doesn't sound like you, Suds," she said.

"They were laughing," I reminded her.

"Are you going to attack everybody who laughs at you the rest of your life?"

"Yeah," I said. "Maybe I will."

I got up from the table and stomped off.

"Take a bath," my mother called.

"I did."

"Take another."

I took another. Didn't do any more good than the first.

I decided to go to bed early. Get myself unconscious as quick as possible. I put on my PJs, turned out the light, and got under the covers. I felt something with my foot. What could be under there? It felt like wood . . . it felt like . . . *SNAP!*

"EEEEEYYYYOWWWWWWWWLLLLLLLL!!!"

Suddenly I was on the floor, and the mouse-trap was on my big toe. I pried it off. I went to the door, yanked it open. I heaved the trap down the hallway. I screamed: "Okay, you *want* a rat, you *got* a rat!"

10
No!

For the next two days, I went on a rampage.

If I saw a little kid with a Twinkie I wanted, I snatched it from him.

If I saw a little kid on a swing, I pushed him off, whether I wanted to use it or not.

I laughed in class during Silent Reading. The teacher told me to stop. I kept laughing. She gave me a detention after school. My first-ever detention. I laughed all through it.

Instead of putting candy wrappers in my pocket, I threw them in the street.

I walked across people's front lawns.

I rang doorbells and ran.

My mother put a new box of Klondike bars in the freezer. I ate them all.

I stuck chewing gum on my bedpost.

I left my dirty clothes on the floor.

The next time Bubba bared his fangs and went, "Wat — wat — wat," I said, "That's my name, badness is my game." And I tied him to the bathroom doorknob.

I snuck up on Zippernose. She was in her room, lying on her stomach on the floor, reading, wearing socks. I pounced. I plunked myself smack on the backs of her legs. In a second I had her socks off.

Most times when I tickled her, I would stop when she started screaming. This time I didn't stop. She laughed and screamed and bawled herself blue.

I didn't stop until my father pulled me off. He shook me by the shoulders. "What's getting into you lately?"

"Nothin'," I said. "Just getting her back."

What *was* getting into me?

Even I didn't know. Didn't care, either. All I knew, whatever it was, it felt good. It felt great.

Why had I waited until so late in life to have my first rampage? Joey was right. Angels finish last. No more last for me. This dude was heading for the gold medal!

I ran upstairs. I pointed at Winky. "You're holding me back," I told him. "You're *outta* here." I opened my window and punted him into the backyard.

There was only one thing left to do.

My chance came next morning.

As I was getting ready for school, my mother poked her head into my doorway. "Pick up this floor before you go," she said. "It's a war zone."

She was already gone from the doorway when I sent my answer: "I don't have time."

She appeared again. "Pardon?"

"I don't have time," I repeated.

"It'll only take a minute. Make time."

"After school," I said.

"Now," she said.

"No," I said.

Before she recovered from the shock, I was past her and down the steps.

"I'll see *you* when you come straight home after school!" she called as I breezed out the door.

The next voice I heard was a whole lot different. I was half a block up the street when I heard it, behind me: "Hi, Suds."

I turned. Not that I had to turn to see who it was. I could have picked Judy Billings' voice out of a million.

She was smiling. She was looking at me. I wasn't a grilled cheese sandwich, after all.

We walked to school together.

Judy did most of the talking. She kept telling me how famous I was. Everybody was talking about me.

But I was only half hearing. I was in a daze. I just kept looking at her beautiful face and thinking, Man! Wow! I'm walking to school with Judy Billings! I don't believe it!

"Well," I heard her say, "could you?"

I snapped out of my daze. "Huh? Could I what?"

"Let a bee sit on your arm, like Joey Peterson did?"

"Sure," I said. "No sweat."

For Judy Billings, I would have let an alligator sit on my arm.

But we couldn't find any bees.

So she said, "How about a spider?"

"Why not?" I said. Playing cool, trying not to sound nervous.

We started searching the gutter and sidewalk and the walls of people's houses. I spotted a couple of spiders, but I didn't say anything.

Then Judy called, "Here! Look!"

It was on somebody's brick wall. It wasn't a little white house spider. It wasn't little and it wasn't white. It was poking along toward a window.

"Just put your hand there, in front of it," Judy said. "Let it crawl right on."

She was excited. Her eyes were wide. Her voice was squeaky.

"Could be a black widow," I said.

"So?" she said. "It won't bite unless you're mean to it."

She was staring at me, waiting. The last ten minutes had been the best ten minutes of my life. Was I going to give it all up because I was too chicken to touch a stupid insect?

I put my hand on the wall, flat. The spider went around it. I did it again. The spider climbed aboard.

Judy shrieked. "Yow!" She pulled on my other arm. "Come on!"

"Where?" I said.

"School! They have to see!"

By the time we got to the school yard, the spider was up around my elbow. A tiny-footed nightmare on my skin.

Judy called: "Look, everybody, *look*!"

Kids came running. They jerked to a stop when they saw. They gasped. They gawked.

"It's a black widow," she announced to them. "He's doing it for me."

The spider was up on my shoulder now, heading for my back. I couldn't see it anymore. I kept my face cool, but I was praying, Please don't go on my neck. *Especially* don't go down my shirt.

The bell rang. Everybody ran for the door. Nobody was looking. I swatted and twisted till I was sure the spider was gone.

At morning recess I was mobbed.

"Wow, Suds!"

"A black *widow*!"

"Black Widow Man!"

"Weren't you *scared*?"

"Ouuuu, Suds!"

Judy was mobbed, too, mostly by girls.

"He did it for *you*?"

I guess we were both famous.

11

What's Wrong with Joey?

Heading for the lunchroom, I grabbed Joey in a headlock. "Hey, brother rat, where you been? Where were you yesterday?"

He pulled out of the headlock. "Home, sick."

I slapped him on the back. "Yo, rats don't get sick," I nudged him. "Know who I walked to school with today?"

"Should I care?"

I pushed him. "C'mon, man, you know. Hey, did you see me with the spider? Huh?"

He shook his head.

"No? Man, you're missing it all." I shook him. "You'd be proud of me." He didn't look too lively. "Hey, brother rat, you still sick?"

We sat at our old spot in the lunchroom.

I plunked my paper bag in front of him. "Notice anything?" He gave a teeny grin. "No more elephants. And look — " I opened up my sandwich. I held it under his nose. "Look familiar?" He turned away. "B-A-L-O-N-Y, baby."

"E-Y," he said.

"Whatever. It's meat, right? M-E-A-T. I feel like I'm about sixteen already. I can feel myself growing." He gave a little snicker-snort. "I ain't kiddin', man. Just sitting here now. Can't you tell? You were right, dude. Don't take nothin'. Number One. I'm doin' it, dude rat." I slapped the table. I ripped off half my sandwich in one bite. "I'm *doin'* it!"

Then I noticed. I grabbed his arms. "Hey, where are they?"

"Where's what?"

"Your tattoos."

He stared at his arms. "Oh . . . uh . . . "

I leaned across the table. I sniffed. "You don't stink. You said you weren't going to take a bath for a month."

"I didn't."

"So where'd the tattoos go?"

"Uh, I sweated. They came off."

"So how come you don't smell?"

"Uh, deodorant."

"And where's your headband?"

"I forgot it."

I finished my sandwich. I started in on my cupcakes. Joey wasn't eating. I pulled his sandwich from his bag. "What kind of meat you got today?"

He snatched the sandwich back. "I don't know."

"Baloney? Roast beef?"

"I don't know."

"Bear? Moose?"

He just glared at me.

"Okay, rat," I said. I stuffed a cupcake into my mouth. When I finally cleared some room for my tongue, I said, "You gotta come over, see my room. It's almost as bad as yours. Oh, man!" I slapped the table. "I almost forgot to tell you. I did it. I did *it*."

He gave me a blank look.

"The *big* one, rat. I said no to my mom. This morning. You shoulda been there. I'm going out to school, okay? My mom says, 'Pick up this floor. It's a war zone.' War zone, man. See. I told you it was bad. So, know what I said? I said, 'I ain't got time.' So she says, '*Make* time.'

And I go, 'No.' N-O, baby, and I'm out the door. I *did* it!''

I held out my hand for him to slap. He didn't slap.

"Know what else? She said, 'Come right home after school.' I'm telling ya, I ain't.'' I scarfed down another cupcake. "I'm thinking, ya know, I gotta get my mom trained, like yours.''

He wasn't talking. He wasn't eating. Nothing. I snatched his sandwich. I shot my chair back so he couldn't reach me. I tore the wrapper off. I opened it. I couldn't believe my eyes. I gawked at him. "*Peanut butter and jelly?* Where's the meat?''

He just stared for another minute. Then he got up and walked away. Left his lunch there, me holding his sandwich. Just walked away.

12

Me and Judy Billings

After school I walked Judy Billings home. She asked if I wanted to come in for a Popsicle. I said sure. I wasn't too anxious to go home anyway, with my mom waiting for me.

As she opened her front door, something gray streaked past my feet.

"Oh, no!" she screeched. "Muffy, get back here! Muf-*feeeee*!"

The cat was already five houses up the street.

Judy stomped her foot. "Ouu, I hate that cat. She always does this."

She slammed the door shut. We took off after the cat.

"Whenever she does this," Judy huffed as we ran, "she goes up a tree."

71

"No sweat," I told her.

Sure enough, two blocks away, there was Muffy, up a tree. Pretty far up. Out on a limb.

Judy slumped. "Oh, no. Here we go again."

"Hey," I reminded her, "I said no sweat."

Hey, I said to myself, you're famous. You're Number One. Judy Billings needs your help. Go for it, Black Widow Man!

I was in luck. The next day was trash pickup day. Cans were out. I dragged one over to the tree. I climbed onto it. It held me. Good.

From the top of the trash can, I looked down at her. She looked up at me, smiling that beautiful smile. I saluted. "See ya."

I was just high enough to get my fingers around the lowest branch. I dug my sneaks into the bark and pulled myself up.

From then on it was easy. One limb after another, and there I was, even with Muffy. "Meow," Muffy said.

"Okay," Judy called from below. "Bring her down."

Down?

For the first time, I looked down.

Uh-oh.

What am I doing up here? How did I get this high?

Far, far below me, the trash can seemed like a thimble. Judy Billings seemed like a doll, her tiny face looking up at me, getting fuzzy, getting wavy. . . .

"Come on, come on," she was saying. Her voice sounded tiny and far away.

I squeezed my eyes shut. I hugged the tree trunk.

"I can't," I said.

"You *can't*?" she called. "Why *not*?"

I tried to think of some other way to say it, but I couldn't. "I'm afraid of heights."

"Oh, *great*," I heard her say. I opened my eyes. Her hands were on her hips. She wasn't smiling anymore.

"I'll probably outgrow it," I said.

"Yeah?" she said. "Well, you'd better outgrow it in the next two seconds, because I want my cat back and I want her back *now*."

Judy, I wanted to say, it's me. Suds. The guy who risked his life with the spider for you.

Something told me it wouldn't make any difference.

Now the tree itself was waving. No way I was going down. I couldn't even look down.

I reached out — out — got the cat in my hand, my hand under it, lifted it from the limb. I prayed

it was right what I had heard, that cats always land on their feet. *Always, please*. I dropped it.

It landed on its feet.

Judy squealed. "Muffy!"

I hugged the trunk again. I scrunched my cheek against the bark, shut my eyes.

When I opened them, only the trash can was beneath the tree. I thought, She's going for somebody to get me down from here.

A long time later, when mothers started calling their kids in to dinner, I changed the thought: She's *not* going for somebody.

I did a bunch of other thinking up there, too. I thought about the little kids I had pushed off swings. About the Twinkies I had snatched. About the spider that probably wasn't a black widow at all. And a girl who was after something, but it wasn't me.

I thought about rats and real men and Number One and angels and fame and first and last and love and nature's way. And for the first time since I started fourth grade, I knew exactly who I was — a scared kid up a tree.

I listened. One of those names being called in for dinner . . . *mine*? One of those mother's voices . . . *mine*!

"Mom!" I yelled. "Here! Up here! Help! Help! Help!" I screamed my lungs out.

Pretty soon my mother appeared. Then my father. Then a ladder.

I came back to earth.

My mother squeezed me harder than I had squeezed the tree. "Look at you," she said. She sounded mad, but I knew she wasn't. "You're shaking like a leaf. What were you *doing* up there?"

I tried to answer, but only tears came out. I blubbered like a baby. I couldn't help it. I didn't care.

I held on tight to my mom as we walked home.

"Sorry I gave you a hard time this morning," I sniveled.

"That's okay,"she said.

"I was trying to be a good rat."

"I know."

I looked up at her. "You do?"

She smiled. "I was talking to Joey's mom."

"Uh-oh."

She laughed.

Ten minutes after we got home, the doorbell rang. It was Joey — and his mother.

"Hi, Suds," said Mrs. Peterson. She was smiling, but Joey, he didn't look so good.

She said, "Joey has something to say to you, Suds."

I thought, What would he want to say to me, especially in front of his mom?

Joey was facing me, but his eyeballs were up in the corners of his eyes. He didn't look any more like Number One than I did.

"I'm, uh, sorry," he said.

"Don't stop there," said his mom.

"I — " Joey blinked, coughed, swallowed, cleared his throat, shifted his feet, and twitched. "I, uh, I'm sorry I got you into — "

"*Pushed* you," said his mom.

" — pushed you into the rat stuff. I shouldn't have talked you into saying no to your mom."

"And what aren't *you* doing anymore?"

"I, uh, I'm not saying no to my mom anymore."

Mrs. Peterson nodded. "Good." She patted Joey on the head. She smiled at me. "Joey also wants you to know that he has dropped out of the rat race and has rejoined the human race."

Mrs. Peterson smiled over my head. My mother was standing behind me. "Guess that'll about do it, Janet."

"I think so," my mom said.

Mrs. Peterson mussed my hair. " 'Bye, Sudsie."

" 'Bye," I said.

They left.

I turned to my mother. "What was all that about?"

"Just what it sounded like," she said. "You didn't really think Mrs. Peterson was going to let him get away with all that nonsense, did you?"

"It *looked* like she was."

She nodded. "You're right about that. She was trying to give him some slack, let him work his way through this rat phase of his."

"That's why she backed off about the tattoos?"

"That's why. Plus she didn't want to discipline him in front of you. But when her patience ran out, that was it. Curtains for Joey the rat."

"He said he was sick yesterday."

She laughed. "It was his mother who was sick. Sick of his shenanigans. She kept him home to clean up his room. *And* his tattoos. *And* his act. So" — she snapped her fingers — "that's that."

For her, maybe.

She was walking away. "Mom," I said, "I have a confession."

13

Confession

My mother turned. Her eyebrows went up. "That so?"

"Yeah," I said. "Maybe Joey did sort of push me. But the last couple days, it was all on my own."

She sat on the edge of the sofa. "I see. Anything else? Confession is good for the soul, you know."

"Well, there was another person in it, sort of."

"I see." She crossed her legs, folded her arms.

"A girl."

She nodded. "Hmm." She thought. "Would her initials be J. B., by any chance?"

I was shocked. "How did you know?"

"You've been in love with Judy Billings since first grade."

How did she know that?

"Well," I said, "something happened with her, and I guess I went a little crazy."

"I see."

"Well, anyway, I think I'm through with her."

My mom nodded. "I imagine she'll survive."

She sat back in the sofa. She just smiled at me for a while.

"Mom?"

"Yes?"

"There's more."

"Is there?"

"Yeah. You know, when I was a rat there?"

"Before you went up the tree?"

"Yeah. Well, I mean, I was *really* a rat. You wouldn't believe it."

"No?"

"I took stuff from little kids. I pushed them off swings. I got a detention at school because I wouldn't stop laughing. I rang doorbells."

"A regular ripsnorter."

"Yeah. And Mom?"

"Yes?"

"It was me that took all the Klondike bars."

Her eyebrows shot up. "*Every* one?"

"Yeah. Totally."

She shook her head. She was dumbfounded. "I'm afraid to ask if there's anything else."

Anything else . . . anything else. Yeah, there *was* something else, something still stuck inside me. What was it? I didn't know.

"Can't think of anything else," I told her.

She reached out and took my hand and squeezed it. "Well, rat or no rat, your mom still loves you."

There!

"Mom, I know now. Something else. When I was being a rat, I thought I was having a great time. But I wasn't. I was having a rotten time." I thought of the faces of the little kids that I had pushed around. "It's like other kids thought I was a big deal or something. But I didn't like myself, Mom." My lip was quivering. "It's no fun being a rat."

My mom's face was blurry as she came toward me and pulled me to her.

We stayed like that for a long time. I heard her sniffling.

After a while she said, "Remember when you said being a rat was the first step to becoming a man?"

"Yeah?"

"Well, I was just thinking. It's kind of funny.

As soon as you stopped *trying* to be a man, you *became* one. In a nice little way, I might add.''

''How's that?''

''Your confession there. Taking blame on yourself. Admitting you were wrong. That's grown-up stuff.''

''Really?''

She hugged me. ''Really.''

''Well,'' I said, ''from now on, I'm just gonna be a kid. That's enough.''

She laughed. ''That's *plenty*!''

Suddenly I remembered. ''Winky!''

I bolted out the back door. I searched the yard. Nothing. I tore the lids off the trash cans. Nothing. Gone. *No!*

My mother's voice came from the doorway. ''We thought you might change your mind.''

I stared at her, at her finger, which was pointing up . . . *upstairs*. . . .

I dashed past her, up the steps, into my room. . . . There he was, my one-eyed teddy bear, sitting on my pillow.

14

Me and Dad

I guess I should mention one other thing to wrap up the story.

It was a couple days later. A Saturday. My dad's day off.

I came back from playing outside and saw him in front of the VCR. I asked what he was watching.

"*E.T.*," he said. Only he didn't say it regular. His voice sounded funny.

I came into the room. I looked at the screen. E.T. was on the table, all white. I looked at my father, at his face. His eyes were glassy. His cheeks were wet.

He was crying!

"Dad — " I said.

He pulled out a hankie and blew his nose. He chuckled. "Every time that little guy dies," he sniffed, "I want to bawl like a baby."

I climbed onto his lap. I hadn't done that for a long time. I nestled into him. "Don't sweat it, Dad," I told him. "I do, too."

About the Author

Jerry Spinelli is the author of several novels, including *The Library Card*, *Picklemania*, and the Newbery Medal–winning *Maniac Magee*. He lives in Phoenixville, Pennsylvania, with his wife and fellow author, Eileen Spinelli, and their children.

Take a Lesson in Laughter

from Newbery Award-winning author Jerry Spinelli

JERRY SPINELLI
Newbery-award-winning author of Maniac Magee

PRINCIPAL

REPORT TO THE PRINCIPAL'S OFFICE

SCHOLASTIC

JERRY SPINELLI
Newbery-award-winning author of Maniac Magee

FOURTH GRADE RATS

SCHOLASTIC